Monique's Favorite Purple Pants

ISBN 979-8-89428-039-4 (paperback)
ISBN 979-8-89428-040-0 (digital)

Christian Faith Publishing
832 Park Avenue
Meadville, PA 16335
www.christianfaithpublishing.com

Printed in the United States of America

Monique's Favorite Purple Pants

Monique Sanders-Phillips and Glenda R Stamps

Today is Monday. It's time to get ready for school. What pants should I wear? I know! My favorite purple pants will save the day. What shirt shall I wear? What shoes will I choose? Well…whatever the choice, one thing is true: as long as I have my favorite purple pants on, any shirt or shoes will do.

I am thinking about the fun day that I'm going to have as I brush my teeth and comb my hair.

"Mom! Where are my favorite purple pants?"

"Your pants are right here, dear. I washed them for you. Hurry and get dressed so you won't be late for school."

Breakfast was yummy and filled my tummy. Now it's time to walk to school with Mom.

"Good morning, Ms. Snow!"

"Good morning, Monique. What pretty purple pants you have on for the first day of the week."

"Thank you, Ms. Snow. Bye, Mom!"

I whisper to Marlene, "I am wearing my favorite purple pants, so I must be careful during our painting lesson."

Oh no! White paint dripped on my favorite purple pants. But that's okay. I'm not worried because Mom will wash the white paint out of my favorite purple pants tonight.

Ding, ding, ding! The school bell rings. It's recess time. I play with my best friends, Brooklyn and Elizabeth. We run, run, run, and jump up high, pretending we are beautiful bluebirds flying in the sky.

Next, we slide down the slide and act silly. Then we chase Tommy, Paul, and Billy.

Ding, ding, ding! The school bell rings. It's time for lunch. Eating lunch with my friends is lots of fun.

Uh-oh! Look what I've done! I spilled milk on my favorite purple pants. But that's okay. It's all right because Mom will wash the milk stains out of my favorite purple pants tonight.

Ding! The school bell rings once. It's time to go home.

Mom meets me at the front gate. She waves, smiles, and gives me a big hug. Then we walk home, laughing and talking about my great day.

I help Mom set the table. We eat baked chicken, macaroni and cheese, and green beans. I play with my toys and my cat, Lily, while Mom is busy washing my favorite purple pants.

Swish, swash, swirl, whirl. I am happy! The washing machine got my favorite purple pants clean.

It's bubble-bath time! Bubbles, bubbles everywhere. I love to blow bubbles in the air. I love the bubbles in my hair. *Splish, splash, splish, splash.* It's time for me to get out of the bath and get ready for bed.

Lily trots down the hall to my room and jumps on my bed. I rub her head. She purrs and lies down at the foot of my bed.

Mom reads me a bedtime story. She kisses me and says, "Good night, Monique. It is time to go to sleep."

I close my eyes, but before I go to sleep, I think, *Hmm… What will I wear tomorrow for school? Ahh-haaa, I know! I'll wear my favorite purple pants.*

About the Authors

Monique Sanders-Phillips

Monique Sanders-Phillips was born in San Francisco, California, and raised in Sacramento, California. She has one amazing daughter. She is a graduate of Sacramento City College with an associate degree in social sciences. She always had a love for writing, acting, and dancing. She performed in one-act plays at Sacramento City College such as "Soap Opera" and "The DMV One" and was a stage manager for "The Accountant." She also performed in various musicals and plays at church. She is also a model for a model agency located in San Francisco, California. In Monique's spare time, she enjoys riding bikes and skating with her daughter.

Glenda R. Stamps

Glenda R. Stamps is a retired licensed vocational nurse, a wife, a mother of four adult children, and one step daughter, a grandmother of eight, and a great-grandmother of one. She was born in San Francisco, California, and reared in Daly City, California. She loved the climate in Sacramento, California, so she relocated there in 1980. Glenda graduated from Sacramento City College with an associate degree in art. Her favorite artistic media are gouache paint, acrylic paint, and pastels. She is also an entrepreneur, "Lips" cosmetics. She enjoys creative writing, reading all types of literature, theatrical plays, and spending quality time with family.